It was a beautiful day.
"I want to go to the park,"
said Jon.
Odie wanted to go, too.
Garfield wanted to sleep.
"You are so lazy, Garfield,"
said Jon.

They all went to the park.
"This is a good place to play,"
said Jon.
"This is a good place to sleep,"
said Garfield.

"Slide, Garfield!"
said Jon.
Garfield would not slide.

"Catch, Garfield!"
said Jon.
Garfield would not catch.

"All you do is sleep,"
said Jon.
"You never play.
Odie and I will play.
We will have fun."

"Wake me for lunch,"
said Garfield.
And he went to sleep.

Later Garfield woke up.
He was hungry.
He saw a boy.
The boy had balloons
and ice cream.
"Ice cream is a good lunch,"
thought Garfield.

Garfield tried to look hungry.
"You are a nice kitty,"
said the boy.
"Here is something for you."

The boy gave Garfield the balloons.
"Not the balloons!"
said Garfield.
"Oh, no!"

Garfield went up, up, up!
He flew over the trees.
"This is fun," thought Garfield.

He flew around
tall buildings.

He flew near the airport.
"I am tired of all this fun,"
thought Garfield.
"How do I get down?"

Garfield was very hungry.
"This looks good," he said.
"It looks like candy."

Garfield made a face.
"It looks like candy.
But it tastes like fuzz."

A bird landed on Garfield.
"What's up, Cat?" he asked.
"I am," said Garfield.
"And I want to go down."

Other birds came to visit.
"How do I get down?"
asked Garfield.
"Let go of the balloons,"
said one bird.
"You are a fat cat.
You will bounce."
The birds laughed.

"This is fun,"
said another bird.
"We can stay here all day."
"Good," said Garfield.
"Now I will have dinner."
The birds did not stay
for dinner!

Garfield was tired.
He was hungry.
His arms were weak.
Garfield let go of the balloons.
He did not mean to!
He fell through the air!

But he had a good landing!
"May I ride along?"
asked Garfield.

Garfield rode with the man.
They landed on the ground.
They landed in the park!
"That was fun," said Garfield.
"Thanks for the ride."

Jon and Odie came back.
Garfield was right where
they had left him.
"You are so lazy," said Jon.
"You did not play today.
Odie and I played.
We had fun."

Garfield smiled.
"I had fun, too.
I had *too* much fun!"
And Garfield fell fast asleep.

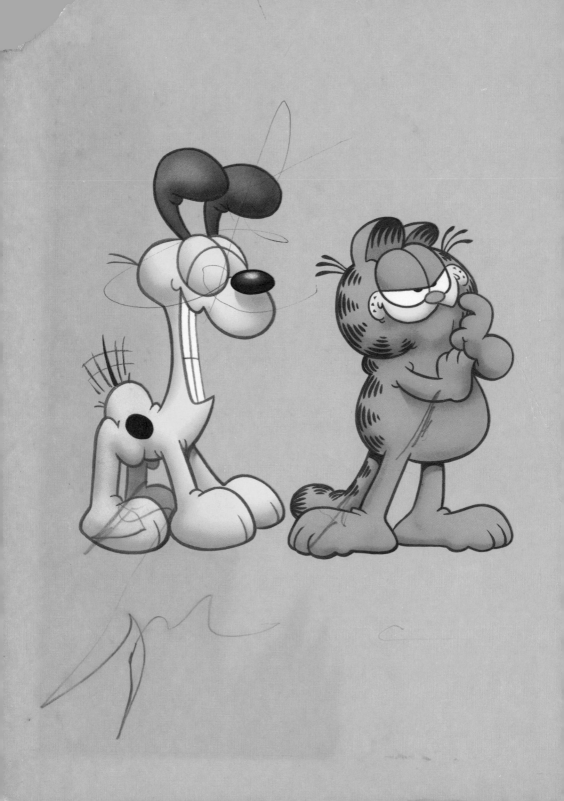